Bad, Bad Cats

Some other books by Roger McGough

Poetry

AN IMAGINARY MENAGERIE
LUCKY
NAILING THE SHADOW
PILLOW TALK
SKY IN THE PIE
YOU TELL ME (*with Michael Rosen*)

Poetry for older readers

YOU AT THE BACK
STRICTLY PRIVATE (Ed.)

Fiction

THE GREAT SMILE ROBBERY
STINKERS AHOY!
THE STOWAWAYS

Contents

Writing the poems
Was great fun to do
Now they need reading
So OVER TO YOU!

The Cats' Protection League

Midnight. A knock at the door.
Open it? Better had.
Three heavy cats, mean and bad.

They offer protection. I ask, 'What for?'
The Boss-cat snarls, 'You know the score.
Listen man and listen good

If you wanna stay in the neighbourhood,
Pay your dues or the toms will call
And wail each night on the backyard wall.

Mangle the flowers, and as for the lawn
A smelly minefield awaits you at dawn.'
These guys meant business without a doubt

Three cans of tuna, I handed them out.
They then disappeared like bats into hell
Those bad, bad cats from the CPL.

Fur Exchange

'Kitten gone missing?
   Ain't that a shame.
Dog next door
   Maybe he's to blame?

Twenty-ton truck
   Charging down the street
Maybe the kitten
   Got under its feet?

Remember that gale
   The other day?
A pity if kitty
   Was blown away.

Foxes, badgers
   Weasels, crows
It's a wicked world
   Every creature knows

Especially the boys
   From the CPL.
By the way, your kitten
   Is it tortoiseshell?

It is? Then recognize
    This piece of fur?
You don't say,
    It could be her?

Well isn't it just
    Your lucky day
That we three happened
    To be passing this way?

Here's our card
    Just give a ring
If you want her back.
    And here's the sting:

We charge a fiver
    For returning kittens
Or else it's a pair
    Of tortoiseshell mittens.'

Mafia Cats

We're the Mafia cats
   Bugsy, Franco and Toni
We're crazy for pizza
   With hot pepperoni

We run all the rackets
   From gambling to vice
On St Valentine's Day
   We massacre mice

We always wear shades
   To show that we're meanies
Big hats and sharp suits
   And drive Lamborghinis

We're the Mafia cats
   Bugsy, Franco and Toni
Love Sicilian wine
   And cheese macaroni

But we have a secret
   (And if you dare tell
You'll end up with the kitten
   At the bottom of the well

Or covered in concrete
   And thrown into the deep
For this is one secret
   You really must keep).

We're the Cosa Nostra
   Run the scams and the fiddles
But at home we are
   Mopsy, Ginger and Tiddles.

(Breathe one word and you're cat-meat. OK?)

A Night on the Tiles

'Mummy, where's Mopsy
    Did she come home last night?
There was thunder and lightning
    Do you think she's all right?

What does she get up to
    Where on earth can she go?
Has she a boyfriend do you think
    A handsome young beau?

Has she a family of kittens
    Is she somebody's wife?
Could our Mopsy be leading
    A strange double life?

(And talking of strange . . .
    Don't you find it funny
That the cushion in her basket
    Is stuffed with money?

Sunglasses? A black trilby?
    Does she wear them for fun?
But two pistols and a loaded
    Sub-machine-gun?)

Mummy, there's a policeman
   Approaching the door
Whatever can a policeman
   Be wanting us for?

With a black plastic bag
   That he's holding so tight.
Mummy, where's Mopsy
   Do you think she's all right?'

Curtains

'Mummy, wasn't he a kind policeman
    collecting jumble for the sale
to raise money for new curtains
    to hang in the city jail?

He liked the old toys that I gave him
    and the games that I've outgrown
even jigsaws with missing pieces
    and the balloons that I've outblown.

And Mopsy's dressing-up clothes
    he thought were really nice
and although the firearms surprised him
    he said they'd fetch a good price.

Mummy, why is he keen to meet Mopsy?
    What does "Help with our inquiries" mean?
I think she has some explaining to do
    Just where has that naughty cat been?'

Vamoose

Dear Franco and Toni

By de time you read dis
I will have vamoosed,
Couldn't face no spell
in de cooler, so I scat.

An old buddy of mudder's
helped me stow away
on dis cruise-bucket
bound for Honolulu.

When we hit de Big Apple
Yours truly gonna jump ship
head straight for de East Side
and join de Mob.

You can betcha nine lives
I soon be de Catfather
and when I'm in de gravy
I'm gonna send for you guys.

       meow and ciao

       Bugsy

Waxing Lyrical

I polish the dining-room table
Bring a shine to the bentwood chairs
You can see your face in the wardrobe
Mind you don't slip on the stairs

I polish the eggs in the kitchen
The bread before I toast it
Cover the chicken with elbow grease
And rub before I roast it

I polish my grandfather's trousers
(At the knees, where he likes them to shine)
My grandmother's nose, how it sparkles!
And her dentures, aren't they divine?

I polish the flowers in the garden
The front of the house, brick by brick
If the clouds would stand still for a minute
I'd wipe the dust off right quick

I polish the car every Sunday
I polish the Sunday as well
I polish the years, and the yearnings
I polish the fears and the smell

I polish the reasons for living
I polish the truth and the lies
I polish your innermost secrets
I polish the earth and the skies.

I polish the language of angels
The horn of the unicorn too
If you think this poem is rubbish
Then I'll call round and polish off you!

Concise Hints for New Teachers

1) If you get lost on your way to school,
   don't ask children for directions.
   (They may be dangerous.)

2) Think twice about wearing the jacket
   you imagined was trendy when you were
   a student.

3) Leave Teddy at home.
   (Yes, I know he misses you.)

4) On your first morning, don't confuse
   the Head Teacher with the Caretaker.
   The Caretaker will never forgive you.

5) If someone shouts in the corridor,
   'Get into line and stop slouching,
   you scruffy article,'
   they are probably not shouting at you.

6) It is all right to enter the staff-room without
   knocking, and the staff toilet is no longer
   out of bounds.

7) If you confiscate the *Beano* in class,
   don't be seen swapping it for bubblegum
   with the P.E. teacher.

8) On Open Night, if one of the parents shouts
   at you, don't burst into tears.
   (Just make a note of the name
   and get your own back on the child later.)

9) Practise scratching your nail down the blackboard –
   the kids will hate it.

10) Bring sandwiches.

Plague Around

There's a plague around
There's a plague around
In every village
And every town

With big purple spots
And greenish ones too
There's a plague around
And it's waiting for you

There's a plague around
There's a plague around
Keep your eyes open
And don't make a sound

Or your ears will flap
And you'll start to cough
You'll sneeze and sneeze
Till your nose drops off

There's a plague around
There's a plague around
In every school
There's a playground

You'll burst out laughing
And run around
When you get into
the playground

There's a playground
There's a playground
In every school
There's a playground.

Here Come the Dinner Ladies

Here come the Dinner Ladies
   One-two-three
Stale rolls for you
   Doughnuts for me

        Sausages floating in custard
          Half-chewed chunks of old meat
        Last week's jam roly-poly
          Stuffed with greasy pigs' feet
              (All for You)

Here come the Dinner Ladies
   One-two-three
Sour plums for you
   Strawberries for me

        Half a roast chicken with French fries
          A pizza freshly made
        Baked apple served with ice-cream
          And loads of lemonade
              (All for Me)

Here come the Dinner Ladies
   One-two-three
Granny, my mum
   and Aunty Vee.

A Weak Poem

(To be read lying down)

Oh dear, this poem is very weak

It can hardly stand up straight

Which comes from eating junk food

And going to bed too late.

Born to Bugle

He was born to bugle
To be a bugler-boy
Not a teddy bear or a bouncy ball
But a bugle his first toy

He bugled before breakfast
In the bath-tub and in bed
And in between he practised
Bugling on his head

He bugled on his bicycle
He bugled on the bus
At the zoo played boogie-woogie
With a hip hippopotamus

He bugled in Bulgaria
Botswana and Bahrein
Stowed below in cargo
Blowing bugle on a plane

He was born to bugle
Be bugling still today
But a burglar burgled his bugle
and took his breath away

And though we mourn the bugle
We mourn the bugler most
As laid to rest we do our best
To whistle 'The Last Post'.

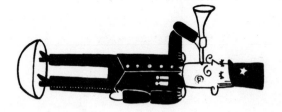

My Brilliant Friend

He's brilliant at karate
He's brilliant at darts
He's brilliant at acting
He gets all the best parts

He's brilliant at swimming
He's brilliant at skates
He's brilliant at juggling
With real china plates

He's brilliant at poetry
He's brilliant at rhyme
He's brilliant at lessons
He comes top every time

He's Brilliant just Brilliant
With a capital B
(Although he's only average
In comparison with me).

Life is a Bucket

(A noisy poem)

Put him in a cave
He'd find a door to slam

Let loose on a cloud
A can to kick

Playing in a haystack
He'd find a plate to smash

Alone on the moon
A balloon to burst

He just can't help it
He's one of those boys

Life is a bucket, so boring
When not filled with noise.

Stonehenge

The plan is simple but will need all our strength.
We have chosen tomorrow because it is the longest day
and darkness will make our task impossible.

Not having our modern learning, our fathers believed
they could simply pluck it from the sky.
Believe me, it will take six hundred of our best men.

TODAY'S VISITOR APPROACHES STONEHENGE ON ITS WEST SIDE.

As soon as the sun rises, as soon as its head
appears above the edge of the land, the net is cast
and the ropes secured before it can take flight.

Laying rollers in front of the sledge, the long haul begins.
Great care must be taken not to scratch its surface
or break off pieces, lest its magic be affected.

THE VISITOR SHOULD NOW PROCEED ALONG THE PATH
AND TURN LEFT TO THE FAR SIDE OF THE CIRCLE.

The cage has cost many lives, may they not be lost in vain.
Once inside, the final stones are raised and a roof
of strongest thatch lowered and made fast.

And there let it sing. For we have him:
The God of light. Giver of warmth and goodness.
All power to us for eternity! Let us make ready.

THE VISITOR SHOULD RETRACE HIS STEPS BY THE SAME ROUTE.

The Magic Skates

I studied a map of the National Trust
And planned a day-long tour
Put my magic skates on
And this is what I saw:

SISSINGHURST and SPEKE HALL
STUDLEY ROYAL and HADRIAN'S WALL
FOUNTAINS ABBEY and LINDISFARNE
MIDDLE LITTLETON TITHE BARN

KINDER SCOUT and GIBBET HILL
GOLDEN CAP and STAINSBY MILL
THE STRANGE SEMI OF MR STRAW
CASTLERIGG and MARSDEN MOOR.

The morning gone already
And still so much to see!
So on I press to ORFORD NESS
No time to stop for tea.

SCOTNEY, RIEVAULX and THE VYNE
RUNNYMEDE and BROOK CHINE
CASTLE COOLE and BLACK GLEN
BRIMHAM ROCKS and WICKEN FEN

THE GIANT'S CAUSEWAY, CROOK'S PEAK
STONEHENGE and FRENCHMAN'S CREEK
HARDY'S COTTAGE and HOPESAY
PULPIT WOOD and PEGWELL BAY.

The poem is nearly over
So, to cut a long journey short,
I reached home, tired but happy
By way of CLEVEDON COURT.

The Concise Guide for Travellers

1)   For covering long distances
          travel is a must.

2)   Destinations are ideal places
          to head for.

3)   By the time you get there
          abroad will have moved on.

4)   To avoid jet lag
          travel the day before.

5)   If you cross the equator
          go back and apologize.

6)   If you meet an explorer
          you are lost.

Tourist Traps

No doubt about it, travel really gets you
out of the house.
I have travelled the lengths and breadths
of most countries too numerous to mention.
China, for instance, I have never been to,
nor that country in Africa
(the one with the foreign-sounding name).
Nearer home though, I have visited Scotland
and bits of Wales.
Remember that when you go abroad,
food prices can be gastronomic,
so eat as much as you can before you leave.
Also, avoid tourist traps.
Should you get your leg caught in one,
scream for help in the local lingo.
On no account bleed,
as this could prove expensive if under-insured.

Weather or Not

The rain that was expected tomorrow
came today.
So the weather is now a day early.

Just think!
If the weather is running 24 hours ahead
what will happen on the Last Day?

Obviously,
having all been used up
there will be no weather.

Spooky, eh?

Fresh

Tomorrow
is being baked
right now.

One More Battle

*Who's that sailor
stern and solemn?*
'Tis Lord Nelson
down from his column.

*Why goes he limping
up the street?*
In search of a long–lost
English Fleet.

*Why driven now
to such despair?*
The need to breathe
some clean fresh air.

Concise Hints for Scuba Divers

1) Before diving in shark-infested oceans
   practise at home in the bath.

2) Make sure the bath is
   free from sharks.

3) While you are at it, check the bath for sting-ray,
   Portuguese men-of-war and the dreaded stone-fish.

4) Don't trust that yellow plastic duck.

5) To be on the safe side,
   practise on the carpet in the living-room.

Film

Went to the cinema
Friday.
Tried to leave before
the end.

Couldn't get out.
It was a cling film.

Busy Diary

I have such a busy diary:
Lunches, gallery openings,
Fashion shows, plays.

It's always off somewhere.
In fact, I haven't seen
My diary for days.

Moan

The sun's too hot and the moon's too cold
The clouds are too young and the stars too old
The Queen's too kind and the King's too grumpy
The pillow's too soft and the bed's too lumpy
The pig's too bare and the lamb's too fleecy
The stew's too thin and the soup's too greasy
The sea's too wet and the beach is too stony
The poem's too long and the poet's too moany!

4-eyes

I went to the optician's and read
A sign in the window which said:
'Free eye-tasting'. I fled.

The Drill of It All

The dentist drilled my teeth
Left right left right

But he didn't do it right
Left right left right

So I've only got one left
Right left right left.

A Gottle of Geer

(To be read aloud without moving the lips)

I an a little wooden dunny
With a hand inside ny gack
How I niss ny daddy and nunny
Now the future's looking glack

Locked all day in a suitcase
I seldon see the sun
I've never tasted lenonade
Or a guttered hot cross gun

The owner takes ne out at night
To sit on his gony knee
He talks a load of ruggish
I think you will agree

Gut the audience go gananas
'Gravo!' 'Gravo!' they cheer
As he drinks a glass of water
And I say: 'A bottle of beer.'

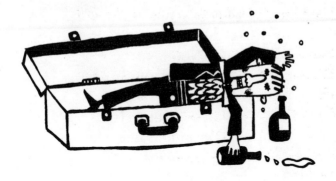

5 Ways to Stop Snowmen Raiding the Fridge

1) Throw banana skins on the kitchen floor.

2) Hang hot-water bottles everywhere.

3) Fill the fridge with smelly socks.

4) Hire a bouncer.

5) Move to the Caribbean.

Train Train

'One two and step
and lift and groan
and two and pull
and sweat and moan

and in and out
and up and breathe
and, oh it hurts
so now I know

it does me good
and three and four
and pull and I
can't wait to see

how much the flab
has gone and two
and step and groan
and sweat and moan

and how I love
the buzz I get
from sweating in
a public place

and pull and stretch
and three and four
how I adore
the pain the pain the

Train with a stranger, train with a trainer
Train Train it's the only way
Train in the morning Train in the evening
Train Train every day

Ah, my station. Excuse me, this is where I get off.
Excuse me, excuse me . . .'

Smalling the Block

He jogged
around the block
so often
he finally
wore it away.

Nursery Slopes

My first morning
  on the nursery slopes

Did I like it?
  I did not

Swerved to avoid
  a rocking-horse

And crashed
  into a cot.

Three Young Rats

Three young rats in satin suits
  Three young cats in leather boots
    Three young ducks in gaberdines
     Three young dogs in denim jeans
      Went out to walk with two young pigs
       In miniskirts and orange wigs
        But suddenly it chanced to rain
         And so they all went home again.

Didgeridoo

Catfish
take catnaps on seabeds
Sticklebacks
stick like glue
Terrapins
are terrific with needles
But what does a didgery do?

Bloodhounds
play good rounds of poker
Chihuahuas
do nothing but chew
Poodles
make puddles to paddle in
But what does a didgery do?

A puffin
will stuff in a muffin
A canary
can nearly canoe
Humming-birds
hum something rotten
But what does a didgery do?

Tapeworms
play tapes while out jogging
Flies
feed for free at the zoo
Headlice
use headlights at night-time
But what does a didgery do?

What does a didgery
What does a didgery
What does a didgeridoo?

We're All Going to the Zoo

We're all going to the zoo
The chimp and the lion
and the kangaroo

The polar bear, the tiger
and the elephant too
We're all going to the Zoo

Boo Hoo Boo Hoo Boo Hoo!

Ticklish

When is a
stickleback
ticklish?

When it's
tickled
with a
little stick
of liquorice.

Picklish

Onions are picklish
Cucumbers too
A dish is delicious
with jellyfish stew

Are donuts picklish?
Don't be ridicklish.

5 Ways to Stop Grizzly Bears from Spoiling Your Picnic

1)   Shoe them away.

2)   Lend them your teddy bears to play with.

3)   Have food that Grizzly Bears don't like
         (e.g. Fish heads . . . Donkey drops . . .
         Rat toenails . . . Frog eyes . . . Pig whiskers . . .
         Baboon bellybuttons . . . Bat milk . . .).
         Definitely NOT Honey!

4)   Have the picnic in a country
         where there aren't any Grizzly Bears:
         South America for instance.
         (But watch out for tarantulas, crocodiles,
         boa constrictors, giant hamsters and child-
         eating goldfish!)

5)   Learn a few Grizzly Bear phrases, like 'Grrr'[1]
         and '*Grr Grr*'[2] and '*G R R R R R R*'.[3]

[1] 'Good Afternoon.'
[2] 'I'm sorry, this is a private picnic.'
[3] 'Scram, or I shall call the armed militia.'

A Cat I Know

A cat I know
who lives in Barnes
can cook and sew
and frequently darns

Much in demand
by the WI
for her catnip sponge cake
and mouse mince pie.

Chutney

A gastronomical cat from Putney
Concocted a wonderful chutney
Bits of old lamb mixed with strawberry jam
Which tasted sweet and yet muttony.

Marmalade

A ginger tom
name of Marmalade
shaved his whiskers
with a razorblade

Last mistake
he ever made.

The Tingling Ground

Play on young friend
Leap and bound
Roll on around
The tingling ground

Bite and scratch
And act real clawful
Before the vet
Does something awful.

5 Ways to Spot the Real Witch at a Hallowe'en Party

1) Tweak everybody's nose.
   (But beware, she may be wearing a false one too!)

2) Taste everybody's 'Newt and Rat-tail stew'.
   (But beware, she may have brought a
   delicious trifle instead!)

3) Test-drive everybody's broomstick.
   (But beware, her real one may be parked
   on the roof!)

4) Stroke everybody's cat.
   (But beware, hers, being the slyest, may
   be the friendliest!)

5) Say in a loud, clear voice:
   'The spinning-wheel belonging to my great-
   grandmother, who was once a beautiful
   princess, has broken down. Can anybody
   mend it?'

   (Beware the volunteer!)

Monstrance

He is neither big nor strong
But his four-year-old thinks he is

She runs towards him, arms outstretched,
And is lifted up into the sky

Five times a week, in little suburbia,
He blazes like a tree.

Why Trees Have Got It All Wrong

Trees have got it all wrong
because they shed their leaves
as soon as it gets cold.

If they had any sense
they'd take them off in June
and let the scented breezes

whiffle through the branches
cooling the bare torso.
In high-summer, more so.

      ★   ★   ★

Come autumn (not the fall)
they'd put on a new coat:
thick leaves, waxed and fur-lined

to keep them warm as toast,
whatever the weather.
Trees, get it together!

A Knight on a Glass Mountain Bike

A knight on a glass mountain bike,
    Came riding down the track
His sword, unsheathed, was crimson
    His armour it was black.

She saw the madness in his eyes
    As he pedalled forth to strike
So picking up a pebble
    She hurled it at the bike.

It shattered, and splinters sent
    The light cascading fountain-like.
The lady smiled, having spent
    The knight on a glass mountain (bike).

Trying to Get Blood out of a Stone

First, I scratched it with my nail
then took a pin
Bent it
trying to stick it in

Squeezed and squeezed
until my hands were sore
Lost my temper
and threw it to the floor

'I'll draw blood' I said
with one last try
Took an axe
and swung it high

The stone shattered
a splinter pierced my face
The blood ran hot
stitches were needed

I tried to get blood out of a stone
x marks the spot
where I succeeded.

5 Ways to Keep Vampires out of Your Bedroom

1)   Before going to bed, brush your teeth
      with garlic toothpaste.

2)   Wash your hands and face with garlic soap.
      (Not forgetting behind your ears,
      and the tender parts of your young and tasty neck.)

3)   Wear that old pair of Superhero pyjamas.
      (OK, OK, so they're too small,
      but who's worried about looking good,
      we are talking life and death here.)

4)   Keep a stake, freshly sharpened,
      under the pillow.

5)   When you hear the first
      fluttering against the
      windowpane, go and
      sleep in the kennel with
      the Rottweiler.

The Suit

Never thought much about fancy clothes
Until I bought myself a field.
It looks real good. Decent soil.
Plenty of room in which to grow.

I walk down the street now
And folks turn round and say, 'Hey,
There goes the feller who wears a field.'

The Sting

This poem has a sting in the tail
Forewarned is forearmed
Those who loiter, alone and pale
Need not be alarmed.

They need not be alarmed
Those who loiter, alone and pale
Forewarned is forearmed
This sting has a poem in the tail.

Misspelt Youth

As a poet I'm a duckling
Who dreams of being a swan
For though my rhymes are sparkling
My speling lets me dwon.

A Well-known Phrase
or Saying

A well-known phrase or saying is:
'A well-known phrase or saying'.

A Well-known Phrase
or Saying

'A well-known phrase or saying'
Is a well-known phrase or saying.

Daffodils

Wandering along the road
By the lake, I saw a load
of golden daffodils
Ten thousand, give or take.

Now and then,
I think of them again.

A certain teacher of English has accused me of plagiarizing a poem
about daffodils by William Wordsworth. I can honestly say that I
have never heard of William Wordsworth nor read his poem
(which is much longer than mine anyway).

A Great Poem

This poem is great.
Wondrous and fabulous
it can hardly wait

to get out there
among you all
and give it to you straight.

If it were a painting
they would hang it
in the Tate.

It's lyrical
It's musical
Intellectually first-rate

Five-Six-Seven-Eight
What do we appreciate?
This poem.

(Who says it's great?)

Roger McGough

3 Ways to Stop Alligators from Biting Your Bottom When You are on the Toilet

1)   Do not go during the rainy season.

2)   If you must go, use only toilets in the first class sections of aeroplanes.

3)   Using face paints, make your bottom so scary it will frighten them away.

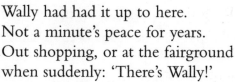

Where's Wally?

Wally had had it up to here.
Not a minute's peace for years.
Out shopping, or at the fairground
when suddenly: 'There's Wally!'

On a crowded beach or busy airport:
'There's Wally!' A giant finger
crushing him into the ground.

He had tried to escape, of course.
Even travelled back through time.
But a finger would wriggle its way
through the holes in history:
'I've found him! There's Wally!'

Finally, he snapped. Gave the rucksack,
sleeping-bag and walking-stick to Oxfam.
The red and white striped jersey
and bobble-hat he burned.
(They were disgusting anyway,
all those dirty finger marks.)

With the money he made from the sale
of the snorkel, camera and binoculars,
he bought contact lenses, a range of
disguises, and a Colt Magnum .45
with a silencer.

Get the picture?
He's out there waiting, over the page
on the next double spread.
The wrong finger in the wrong place
at the wrong time – 'There's Wally!'
          And Phffft!
                    You're dead.

Late-night News

Sorry, there's nothing new to say
It's all been said before
The slaughter of the innocents
The futility of war.

The empty streets, the rifle shots
The corpses not yet cold
The interviews with colonels
Who say as they are told.

The refugees, the loaded carts
The feeble and the lame
Locations change from week to week
But the misery's the same.

A million miles of footage
Countless reels of tape
Twentieth-century history:
Murder, torture, rape.

When we hear the starting gun
We dispatch the nearest crew
Today it's Sarajevo
Tomorrow? A town near you.

So if you wake up screaming
From dreams you did not choose
Remember that you saw it first
Here on late-night news.

The House

Goodbye house –
It's been great
Crooked chimney
Creaking gate

Comings and goings
Of friends and cats
Cuddles and kisses
Occasional spats

Two wee girls
Up and flown
Now he's gone
I'm alone

Goodbye house –
Hello Home!

The Going Pains

Before I could even understand
The meaning of the word 'command'
I've had them. The going pains.

Go to your room
Go to bed
Go to sleep

Twinges that warned of trouble in store
And once in the classroom, the more
I felt them. The going pains.

Go to the back
Go and start again
Go to the Headmaster

From year to year I hear it grow
The unrelenting list of GO.
That bossy word that rhymes with NO
Still can hurt. The going pains.

Go
Go now
Why don't you just go.

What She Did

What she did
was really awful
It made me feel quite ill
It was wrong and quite unlawful
I feel queasy still.

What she did
was quite uncalled for
How could she be so cruel?
My friends were all appalled, for
she made me look a fool.

What she did
was out of order
It made me blush and wince
From that instant I ignored her
and haven't spoken since.

What she did
was really rotten.
But what it was
I've quite forgotten.

Penultimate Poem

Pen ultimate
She said
So I wrote:
The End.

The Reader of This Poem

The reader of this poem
Is as cracked as a cup
As daft as treacle toffee
As mucky as a pup

As troublesome as bubblegum
As brash as a brush
As bouncy as a double-tum
As quiet as a sshhh . . .

As sneaky as a witch's spell
As tappy-toe as jazz
As empty as a wishing-well
As echoey as as as as as as . . . as . . . as . . .

As bossy as a whistle
As prickly as a pair
Of boots made out of thistles
And elephant hair

As vain as trainers
As boring as a draw
As smelly as a drain is
Outside the kitchen door

As hungry as a wave
That feeds upon the coast
As gaping as the grave
As GOTCHA! as a ghost

As fruitless as a cake of soap
As creeping-up as smoke
The reader of this poem, I hope,
Knows how to take a joke!

Carnival of the Animals

Based on the musical burlesque written by Camille Saint-Saëns, which was first performed in 1886

The Royal March of the Lion

Attention everybody
   Pray silence in the hall!
His majesty the lion
   Is about to pay a call.

Isn't he magnificent?
   Doesn't he take one's breath away?
Aren't we pleased to bow before him?
   Isn't this our lucky day?

Isn't he remarkable?
   So strong, so fierce, so proud.
Let us sing his praises.
   Let us sing them long and loud:

   O guzzler of gazelles
   O shredder of zebras
                 We fear thee.

   O cruncher of girafflets
   O short-shrifter of zookeepers
                 We steer clear of thee.

O caliph of carnivores
O shah of savagery
We stay downwind of thee.

O nabob of gnawed bones
O potentate of pot roast
May thy belly be ever full.

Relax everybody
    Leo's out of hearing
Feel free to breathe
    a sigh of relief

But no clapping please
    or cheering
In case he hears
    and charges back

All claws and teeth
    and roaring.
The supercilious psychopath.
    Lion Kings, aren't they boring?

Cocks and Hens

The Hens

Aren't we the lucky ones, we hens?
  We've got it made.
Laying eggs for pleasure
  And once they're laid . . .

Life is a doddle
  With little to do
The occasional cuddle
  And then muddle through.

Corn falls from heaven
  The hen-house is cosy
All clucking and chuckling
  Fine-feathered and rosy.

We've said it before
  And we'll say it again
No life could be finer
  Than the life of a hen.

The Cock

Won't you listen to them cackling on?
    Innocent as day–old chicks.
If they but knew the half of it.
    Mister Fox, for instance, and his filthy tricks.

And the battery prisons in which
    Their relatives are enslaved.
From terrors real and imagined
    My ladies I have saved.

I watch them run around the yard
    Laughing and playing
Protected by a loving shell
    Of my laying.

Asses

Never harass an ass
An ass will never forgive
Compared to an ass, an elephant
Has a memory like a sieve.

For months, maybe years off,
When you've forgotten what you said
He'll burst into your bedroom
And turf you out of bed.

He'll bite your nose and ears off
He'll trample on your head
As you bleed, and plead for mercy,
And you've forgotten what you said.

★   ★   ★

'Not true! Not true!' I hear you cry,
'The ass is the apple of our Lord's eye.'
A sweet old donkey? Perhaps you're right.
(But lock your bedroom door each night!)

Trouble the Tortoise

I'm a teenage tortoise
  A tearaway, a rebel
I live life in the fast lane
  My middle name is Trouble

My parents and their parents
  What dull old lives they lead
They never go out dancing
  They're terrified of speed

In church they sing the praises
  Of slowness and calm
'Best foot backward,' their advice is,
  'And you'll come to no harm.'

But I'm young and impatient
  And I don't easily scare
I've read that fable by Aesop
  And I envy the arrogant hare

A tortoiseshell is tortoise hell
  A heavy cross to bear
If only I could shatter it
  And naked take to the air

Not for me the torture
　Of a future boring and long
So I sing an anthem for doomed youth:
　'Live fast – die young.'

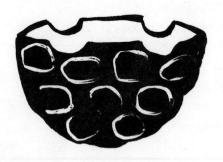

Elephant

If I could be reincarnated
   (And who knows, I might have been already?)
Then I'd like to return as an elephant
   Reliable and steady.

Big as a room filled with sunshine,
   A giant, gentle and strong,
Lord of the manor
   I'd roam the savannah
Trumpeting all day long.

At sunset it's down to the river
   To meet my old pals for a chat
After a few bouts of trunk-wrestling
   We'd squirt water, do daft things like that.

Then tired and happy we'd lumber home
   Humming an elephant tune
Thinking our thanks to our maker
   By the light of an elephant moon.

If I could be reincarnated
   An elephant I would choose,
Failing that, Napoleon,
   Kim Basinger or Ted Hughes.

Sticky Paws

In Australia where the kangaroo roams
    (Or leaps, I suppose I should say)
The creature is found in very few homes
    And is rarely invited to stay.

In supermarket and shopping mall
    They are considered very bad news
Each corner shop, upon the wall
    Has a notice: 'No kangaroos'.

And the reason? They have sticky paws
    Shoplifting is the name of their game
They clear the shelves, empty the drawers
    Filch and pilfer without shame.

When nabbed: 'It's Mother Nature,' they cry,
    'We're designed for carrying swag
We love to thieve and that is why
    We've an inbuilt carrier bag!'

People with Long Ears

People with long ears
   Can hear every little sound:
A butterfly on tiptoe
   Snow settling on the ground

A rose blinking in the sunlight
   The last breath of a bee
The heartbeat of an egg
   Leaves taking leave of the tree

The shimmy of a golden carp
   The hiatus of a hawk
The wriggle of a baited worm
   The bobbing of a cork

The echo in a coral reef
   The moon urging the tide
A cloud changing shape
   They listen, open-eyed.

People with long ears
   Hear such sounds every day
And try to recapture
   In a melodious way

The music that surrounds them
 So isn't it sad to say
That being tone-deaf their chorus
 Is an ear-crunching BRAY.

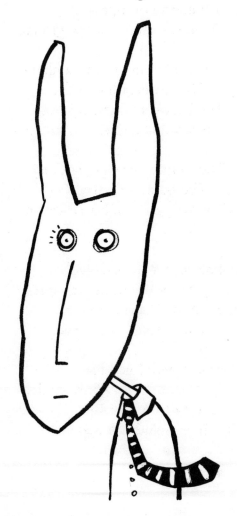

Spring

My mother taught me how to do it.
'As simple,' she said, 'as falling out of a nest.
Think of the word 'spring'. Spring the season,
and the spring that is tightly wound
inside of you. The rest is easy.

Come the day, you'll wake up
with a funny feeling, slightly queasy.
A tickle in the throat. Your heart
racing like never before. Then –
Snap! It's the spring unwinding.'

★   ★   ★

So here I am, one year on
and finding it just like she said.
The heart, the tickle, the senses reeling.
A trigger released, and a coil
unwinding. Spring, the first day!

But what am I supposed to say?
I've clean forgotten the words of the song.
Was it: 'Spring spring'? No, that's wrong.
Oh, this is silly, what am I to do?
Ah, yes, I remember, I sing my name:

'CUCKOO.'

Aquarium

The ocean's out there
   It's vast and it's home
And I want to be in it
   With the freedom to roam

Not stuck in a prison
   That's made out of glass
For humans to peer into
   As they file past

It's all right for goldfish
   And small fry like that
But I deserve more
   Than being ogled at

Imagine the look
   You'd have on your face
If you had to live
   In such a small space

Little wonder
   That I look so glum
Banged up in a seaside
   Aquarium.

Aviary

Beware the canary
gone hairy

Fed on steroids
instead of seeds

On humans now
this mutant feeds

A tweet like thunder
eyes that rage

Do not loiter
near its cage

Beware and be wary
there's nothing as scary
as a furry canary.

Budgerigars
who smoke cigars

In the back
of large Rolls-Royces

Are mere poseurs
who put on airs

And seldom
have fine voices.

Avocet   Blackca**P**
Vulture   Budgeriga**R**
Ivory gull   Kiw**I**
Albatross   Ibi**S**
Razorbill   Cockato**O**
Yellow hammer Hero**N**

The Pianists

Hear the pianists practising their scales
Alongside which all noise-pollution pales

Tangled of finger and languid of wrist
They uncover notes that do not exist

The sliver of sharps, the belly-flop of flats
The skidding of tyres, the squealing of cats

The stuttering staccato, the dumbfounded pause
The pianists hear only tumultuous applause

★　　★　　★

For they are centre stage in a vast concert hall
The recital was tremendous, and they owe it all

. . . to practice.

Putting the piano through its paces
Practice makes perfect. But not in most cases.

Fossils

Fossils are jigsaw-pieces
   That palaeontologists collect
But the picture that emerges
   May be one we don't expect.

For example: Tyrannosaurus Rex,
   Everybody's favourite dinosaur.
Who hasn't been chased out of a nightmare
   By that gigantic beast?
Teeth gnashing, talons flashing,
   Leaping out of Jurassic Park
Into your bedroom as soon as it's dark.

But that illustration on the jigsaw box
   Scientists now admit
Doesn't match the real thing
   Once the fossil pieces fit.

For they claim that old Tyranners
   Was not the monster he appears
Scold him for bad manners
   And he'd burst into tears.

A big softie. A pushover.
   Than fight a triceratops to the death
He'd rather have his tummy tickled
   And laugh until he's out of breath.

After fetching sticks he would roll on his back
   With his feet in the air. Faithful to the end.
A bowl of milk, a few dinosaur biscuits,
   He was Neanderthal Man's best friend.

So T. Rex and T. Regina
   (For let's not be sexist here)
Suffered a grave injustice
   That shortened their career.

So if you want fearsome monsters
   The bloodthirstiest you can find
Forget about the dinosaurs
   Read *The History of Mankind*.

Swans

Swans have class written all over them.
Oh, I could go on and on
About the beauty of the swan.
Aristocracy and no mistake
The way they lord it round the lake.

Poets love them. The bell-beat
Of their wings. The softness of the breast.
Voiceless and safely distant
Where Beauty is at its best.

Poets love them. But not this one.
What others see as graceful elegance
I see as po-faced arrogance.
With a neck like a stunted giraffe
And a beak that glows like a satsuma
You'd think they'd enjoy a good laugh
But they're completely devoid of humour.

For instance: Name a cartoon swan.
Can anybody do swan impressions?
Pull a swan face?
Anybody know any swan jokes?

'I say, I say, I say . . .

'Why won't a swan go on the lake when it's choppy?'

'Because it can't admire its reflection in the water.'

(I was told that one by a duck.)

All that swans are good for
    Is swanning around
Like little girls in pretty dresses
    Imitating doomed princesses.

I speak not in jest
    For there's no denying
That swans are at their best
    On stage, when dying.

Finale

Now finally, the finale
   Which, following the trend
In musical tradition
   Comes firmly, here, at the end.

When all the characters
   That have charmed us
Line up to take a bow
   Wave their hoofs, their paws, their fins
Shout 'Au revoir', 'Adios', 'Ciao.'

They whistle, squeak and trumpet
   They coo and bark and bray
Then disappear into the shadows
   As the last note fades away.

For the carnival is over
   The final page of the score
Thank you all for listening
   Now, maestro please, encore!

Index of First Lines